P9-DXL-141

DETECTIVE PAW OF THE LAW

The Case of the Stolen Drumsticks

Time to Read™ is an early reader program designed to guide children to literacy success regardless of age or grade level. The program's three levels correspond to stages of reading readiness, making book selection straightforward, and assuring that when it's time for a child to read, the right book is waiting.

Beginning to Read

- Large, simple type
- Basic vocabulary
- Word repetition
- Strong illustration support

Reading with Help

- Short sentences
- Engaging stories
- Simple dialogue
- Illustration support

Reading Independently

- Longer sentences
- Harder words
- Short paragraphs
- Increased story complexity

Also by Dosh Archer

Urgency Emergency!

Itsy Bitsy Spider

Big Bad Wolf

Little Elephant's Blocked Trunk

Humpty's Fall

Baaad Sheep

Detective Paw of the Law

The Case of Piggy's Bank

The Case of the Stolen Drumsticks

DETECTIVE PAW OF THE LAW

The Case of the Stolen Drumsticks

Dosh Archer

Albert Whitman & Company
Chicago, Illinois

To Erin

Library of Congress Cataloging-in-Publication data
is on file with the publisher.

First published in the United States of America
in 2018 by Albert Whitman & Company
ISBN 978-0-8075-1556-3

Printed in China
10 9 8 7 6 5 4 3 2 1 WKT 22 21 20 19 18

For more information about Albert Whitman & Company,
visit our website at www.albertwhitman.com.

Prologue

In the heart of Big City is Big City Police Headquarters, home to the Big City Police Force.

This is where Detective Paw works with his assistant, Patrol Officer Prickles.

Detective Paw is logical and determined and has been a detective for a very long time. Detective Paw can outthink any criminal with his brilliant brain.

Patrol Officer Prickles is brave and loyal and has all the latest police-issue crime-fighting gadgets. He goes

for a 5k run every evening. Patrol Officer Prickles is always there to help Detective Paw.

Together they solve crime; that's what they love doing...although it's not always easy.

CRIME
NEVER
PAYS

Chapter One

It was a hot summer afternoon at Big City Police Headquarters, and Detective Paw was just about to have a cup of coffee when his phone rang.

It was Patrol Officer Prickles.

"It's Patrol Officer Prickles here. There has been a robbery at Vinnie 'The Crash' McLaren's apartment,

192B Starr Street! Can you get here as quickly as possible to solve the crime and find the robber?"

"Secure the scene, Prickles," said Detective Paw. "I'll be there shortly."

Detective Paw put down his coffee, grabbed his notebook (for writing down clues) and his magnifying glass (for spotting teeny-tiny clues), and jumped into his old

Vintagemobile. He drove to the scene of the crime.

When he arrived, Patrol Officer Prickles was waiting for him in Vinnie's second-floor apartment.

"The scene is secure, sir," said Patrol Officer Prickles.

"Very good, Prickles," said Detective Paw. "Fill me in on what's happened."

“This is Vinnie,” said Patrol Officer Prickles. “He’s the drummer in a band. His drumsticks have been stolen!”

“My best Classic 5C hickory-wood drumsticks! Gone!” cried Vinnie.

“Tell me what you know,” said Detective Paw.

“I was drumming, and it was so hot

that I got thirsty. I popped out to get some root beers," said Vinnie. "When I came back, I heard someone inside, but when I opened the door, they were gone!"

"So you left the window open?" asked Detective Paw.

"I forgot to close it," said Vinnie.

“Let me know what you’ve got, Prickles,” said Detective Paw.

Patrol Officer Prickles took out his latest police-issue electronic notepad. “I arrived at the scene of the crime at 3:07 p.m. and noted the following:

1. The window was open.

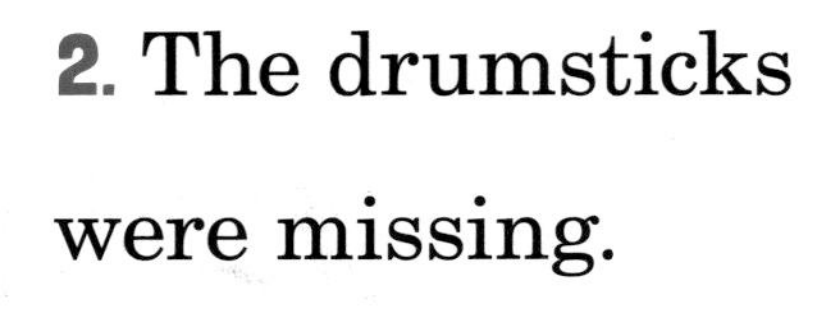

2. The drumsticks were missing.

3. This note was left on the table.”

Detective Paw looked at the note. It read: TOO NOISY ☹.

"We need this as evidence," said Detective Paw.

Patrol Officer Prickles used his latest police-issue high-grade steel tweezers to pick up the note and put it in a plastic evidence bag.

"Well done, Prickles," said Detective Paw. "Good work."

“Why would someone leave that note?” cried Vinnie.

Detective Paw looked at Vinnie’s drum kit.

“That’s a large drum kit,” said Detective Paw.

“You bet!” said Vinnie. “I like my drumming LOUD!”

“Hmm,” said Detective Paw. “That sure is interesting for my investigation.”

“It’s the Battle of the Bands tomorrow,” cried Vinnie. “My band, The Raccoons, is in the finals! How can I play without my best drumsticks?”

Detective Paw loosened his tie and popped a peppermint in his mouth to help him think. “Calm down,” he said. “I will get to the bottom of this.”

Chapter Two

"Who are your neighbors?" asked Detective Paw.

"Below is Mr. Burrows," said Vinnie, "and in the big house next door is Ms. Breevort. She is a writer."

"Thank you," said Detective Paw. "Patrol Officer Prickles and I need to get on with our investigative police duties.

Please go and wait in the kitchen."

"Well, Prickles," said Detective Paw. "Vinnie makes a lot of noise, and this note was left by the person who stole the drumsticks to say they did not like the noise."

"I see," said Patrol Officer Prickles, looking confused.

"The neighbors are the suspects because they can hear Vinnie when he is drumming."

"Why take only the drumsticks?" asked Patrol Officer Prickles.

"To stop Vinnie from drumming and get some peace and quiet," said Detective Paw. "Vinnie might have been more considerate, but stealing is stealing, and we must investigate. First, are there any fingerprints on the note?"

Patrol Officer Prickles went to his car and got his latest police-issue Pro X Fingerprint Kit. He took the note out of the bag with the tweezers and dusted it. There were no fingerprints on it.

"Hmm," said Detective Paw.

“Whoever wrote that note must have been wearing gloves. There won’t be any fingerprints anywhere.”

Detective Paw looked out the window to the grass below. Right beside the window was a large drainpipe coming up from the ground.

“It is possible that someone climbed

up the drainpipe and in through the window," said Detective Paw. "We must search outside."

Outside, under the window, Patrol Officer Prickles scanned the ground with his latest police-issue laser HiVi Groundsearch Scanner. He couldn't find anything.

Detective Paw used his magnifying

glass to look carefully through the grass.

"Aha!" said Detective Paw. "I may

have found another clue!" He held up a pearl earring.

Patrol Officer Prickles put the earring in a plastic evidence bag.

"Okay," said Detective Paw. "Now I must go and interview the neighbors."

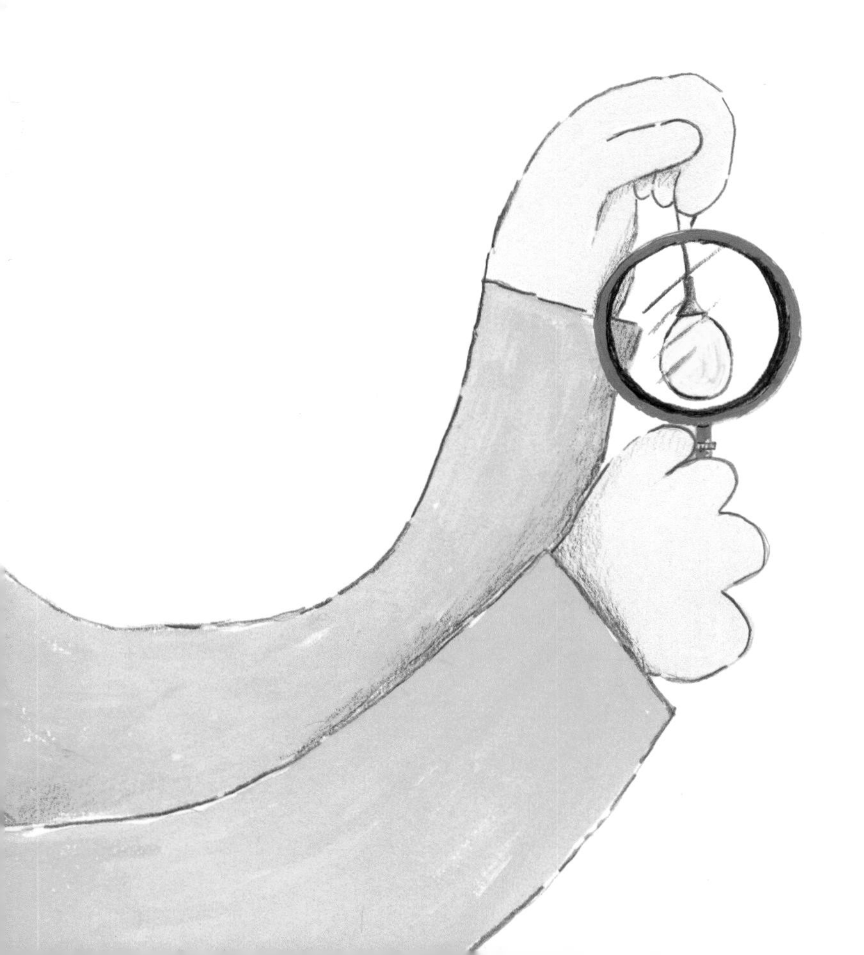

Chapter Three

Detective Paw knocked on Mr. Burrows's door. Mr. Burrows was old, and it took him a while to answer. He was using his walking stick.

"Come in," he said.

"We are investigating a robbery," said Detective Paw. "Can we ask you some questions, please?"

"Go right ahead," said Mr. Burrows.

"Have you ever been disturbed by drumming noises?" asked Detective Paw.

"Yes," said Mr. Burrows, "by Vinnie upstairs. He's a nice boy, and he helps me carry my groceries, but I have to bang on the ceiling with my walking stick to make him be quiet."

“Where were you this afternoon?” asked Detective Paw.

“I was here,” said Mr. Burrows. “On my own, watching the motorcar race. It was very exciting. Someone won!”

“We will be in touch,” said Detective Paw.

They went downstairs.

"Now we need to speak to Ms. Breevort," said Detective Paw.

Ms. Breevort answered her door in a summer dress, a necklace, and gardening gloves.

"Ms. Breevort, we are investigating a robbery. Can you tell us where you were this afternoon?"

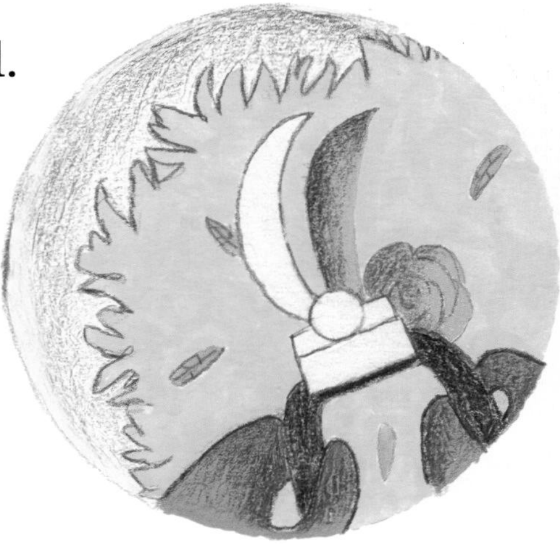

Ms. Breevort sniffed. "Pruning my roses," she said, without inviting them in.

"I see," said Detective Paw. "May I ask, ma'am, have you ever been disturbed by drumming noises?"

Ms. Breevort glared toward Vinnie's apartment.

"That young man certainly makes a lot of noise, especially when I am trying to write...now, I really am VERY busy." She shut the door.

Detective Paw and Patrol Officer Prickles went to sit in Patrol Officer Prickles's car with the air-conditioning on.

"They have all admitted they were disturbed by the drumming," said Detective Paw. "It could be any one of them."

"But *which* one?" asked Patrol Officer Prickles.

"This is a two-peppermint problem,"

said Detective Paw. He popped *another* peppermint into his mouth to help him think extra hard.

After he had thought extra hard, Detective Paw said, "Mr. Burrows is too old to climb up the drainpipe and through the window. But it seemed strange Ms. Breevort didn't invite us in..."

Then Detective Paw looked up and saw smoke coming out of Ms. Breevort's chimney.

"Prickles," said Detective Paw, "I may have just spotted another clue."

Chapter Four

Detective Paw knocked on Ms. Breevort's door a second time. Ms. Breevort opened it and peered out.

Detective Paw looked over her shoulder, into her living room, where he could see a fire in the fireplace!

"Why do you need to have a fire on such a hot day, ma'am?" asked Detective Paw.

"I'm cold," said Ms. Breevort. A bead of sweat trickled down her forehead, and she tucked her hair behind her ears.

It was then Detective Paw noticed she was missing an earring. A PEARL earring. He looked again at the fire and saw the tip of a drumstick before flames flicked over it, turning it to ash.

“You don’t look cold,” said Detective Paw. He held up the bag with the pearl earring. “Do you recognize this?”

Ms. Breevort put her hand to her ear and gasped!

“I have good reason to believe you are the one who committed the robbery,” said Detective Paw. “Ms. Breevort, you are under arrest!”

"Go away!" cried Ms. Breevort. "You have no right to come here. I did the only thing I could to make Vinnie be quiet! I do not like loud noise, it disturbs me when I am writing, and I cannot think of names for my characters!"

"Ms. Breevort!" said Detective Paw. "I am sorry your characters are nameless, but that is no excuse for taking the law into your own hands. You will have to come with us to the station."

They waited for Ms. Breevort to get her handbag, and then they took her to Patrol Officer Prickles's car.

Vinnie and Mr. Burrows had come down and were waiting on the street.

When Ms. Breevort saw Vinnie, she shouted, "I just wanted some peace and quiet, and I would have gotten it if it hadn't

been for these two troublesome cops!"

"How could she have done this?" cried Mr. Burrows.

"How *did* she do it?" cried Vinnie.

"She spotted Vinnie leaving his apartment earlier," said Detective Paw, "while she was pruning her roses, and she took her opportunity. She climbed up the drainpipe and in through his open

window, stole the drumsticks, and came back down the drainpipe. She left a note to show she was fed up with the noise."

"What about my drumsticks?" asked Vinnie.

"She burned them," said Detective Paw. "To get rid of the evidence."

"Aaaaaaaargh!" cried Vinnie. "But it's the Battle of the Bands TOMORROW! I will have to use my second-best pair. They won't be the same."

"Vinnie," said Detective Paw, "I want to talk to you."

“Me?” said Vinnie.

“Yes,” said Detective Paw. “You have to make less noise.”

“But I have to practice,” said Vinnie.

“Practicing is important, but so is being kind to your neighbors and not playing when it will disturb them,” said Detective Paw.

Vinnie sighed. “I understand. I’m sorry for being so loud.”

“From now on you can practice in my garage,” said Mr. Burrows. “It is soundproof and has air-conditioning, so you can keep the windows shut."

"Good idea," said Detective Paw.

Once they were at police headquarters, Detective Paw said to Ms. Breevort, "Taking things that do not belong to you is very serious. I'm only sorry you didn't try to work things out sooner. You could have asked Vinnie to be more quiet or asked us to have a word with him. Instead you resorted to stealing."

"I'm sorry," said Ms. Breevort. "I will buy Vinnie some new drumsticks."

“I was about to suggest that,” said Detective Paw. “But I’m glad you offered.”

Just then the phone rang. Detective Paw picked it up. He nodded and stroked his beard and said, “Thank you, Vinnie. I will let Ms. Breevort know.”

“That was Vinnie,” said Detective Paw to Ms. Breevort. “He isn’t going to press charges. That means you will be allowed to go home today. However, you

will have to come back tomorrow and have some Being-Able-to-Work Things-Out lessons from the Police Peace Officer, Pamela Parker."

"Thank you," said Ms. Breevort, "and I will go to the drumstick shop on my way home."

"Be sure to remember to get the Classic 5C hickory-wood drumsticks," Detective Paw called after her as she left.

Once she was gone, Patrol Officer Prickles said, "Brilliant work, Detective

Paw. How did you figure it out?"

"It wasn't easy," said Detective Paw, "but the clues were there. The note had no fingerprints on it, so whoever wrote it must have been wearing gloves, and when Ms. Breevort answered the door she was wearing gloves. The drainpipe was easy for her to climb. Also there was a note, so it had to be someone who likes to write. Then the pearl earring: it must have fallen off as she climbed through the window. And it was such a hot day, she didn't need a fire, so she must have been burning *something*. Drumsticks are made of wood and burn nicely."

"What will happen to Ms. Breevort?" asked Patrol Officer Prickles.

"Police Peace Officer Pamela Parker is firm but fair, and Ms. Breevort will learn a lot from the lessons," said Detective Paw. "Afterward I will keep an eye on Ms. Breevort to make sure she doesn't try to take the law into her own hands again."

Temperatures had certainly boiled over in this case, but thanks to Detective Paw's detective work and Patrol Officer Prickles's help, they had cooled things down and brought a little bit of peace to Big City.